Dear Parent:
Your child's love of reading st

Every child learns to read in a different way and at his or her own speed. Some go back and forth between reading levels and read favorite books again and again. Others read through each level in order. You can help your young reader improve and become more confident by encouraging his or her own interests and abilities. From books your child reads with you to the first books he or she reads alone, there are I Can Read Books for every stage of reading:

SHARED READING
Basic language, word repetition, and whimsical illustrations, ideal for sharing with your emergent reader

BEGINNING READING
Short sentences, familiar words, and simple concepts for children eager to read on their own

READING WITH HELP
Engaging stories, longer sentences, and language play for developing readers

READING ALONE
Complex plots, challenging vocabulary, and high-interest topics for the independent reader

I Can Read Books have introduced children to the joy of reading since 1957. Featuring award-winning authors and illustrators and a fabulous cast of beloved characters, I Can Read Books set the standard for beginning readers.

A lifetime of discovery begins with the magical words **"I Can Read!"**

Visit www.icanread.com for information
on enriching your child's reading experience.

Library of Congress Control Number: 2020950535
ISBN 978-0-06-306069-2

22 23 24 25 LSCC 10 9 8 7 6 5 4 3 2 ❖ First Edition

I Can Read!

BEGINNING 1 READING

my LiTTLE PONY

Welcome to Ponyville

HARPER

An Imprint of HarperCollinsPublishers

Welcome to Equestria!

Equestria is a world

full of ponies.

This is a map of Equestria.
There are so many
great places to visit.

In the center of Equestria

is the busy town of Ponyville.

Ponyville is a place where all kinds
of ponies live together in harmony.

Ponyville is the heart of Equestria.

It is full of the best ponies around!

There is a group of ponies
called the Mane 6.
They are best friends
who live in Ponyville.

The town square is in

the center of Ponyville.

The ponies gather

in the town square

for important events.

Near the town square

is the Castle of Friendship.

Princess Twilight Sparkle
lives there with Spike.
Spike is a young dragon.
He is Twilight's best friend.

Spike helps Twilight with everything!
He even helps her find
books to read for fun!

Twilight loves to read.

She even started her own school!

It's called the School of Friendship.

After visiting the school,

you may want to do

some shopping.

Luckily, Rarity owns the
Carousel Boutique.
It's located right in Ponyville!

At the Carousel Boutique,
your fashion dreams
will come true.

Take a look at Rarity's designs.

They are perfect for any

pony party!

After shopping, visit
Sweet Apple Acres.

This is where a lot of

the food in Ponyville is grown.

Try a yummy apple!

Applejack and her dog

help on the farm.

Applejack often sells the apples
at the Ponyville market!

Next, let's visit a place made
of clouds and rainbows.
The Cloudominium floats
over Ponyville.
It's where Rainbow Dash lives.

You can also visit

this cute cottage.

It's just outside Ponyville.

It's Fluttershy's cottage.

She lives there with

her bunny, Angel!

Fluttershy's cottage is at the edge
of Everfree Forest.
That is where she plays with Angel
and her butterfly friends.

It's the perfect place for anypony who likes peace and quiet.

If you like fun and treats,
then visit Sugarcube Corner!
This bakery has any dessert
you could ever want.

Pinkie Pie will be sure to make your treat extra sweet!

The ponies love when
friends stop by to visit.
Come back soon!